Pebble® Plus

Under the Sea

Manatees

WITHDRAWN

by Jody Sullivan Rake

Consulting Editor: Gail Saunders-Smith, PhD

Consultant: Debbie Nuzzolo, Education Manager
SeaWorld, San Diego, California

Capstone press®

Mankato, Minnesota

Pebble Plus is published by Capstone Press,
151 Good Counsel Drive, P.O. Box 669, Mankato, Minnesota 56002.
www.capstonepub.com

Books published by Capstone Press are manufactured with paper
containing at least 10 percent post-consumer waste.

Library of Congress Cataloging-in-Publication Data
Rake, Jody Sullivan.
    Manatees / by Jody Sullivan Rake.
    p. cm.—(Pebble Plus. Under the sea)
    Summary: "Simple text and photographs present manatees and their lives under
the sea"—Provided by publisher.
    Includes bibliographical references and index.
    ISBN-13: 978-0-7368-6723-8 (hardcover)
    ISBN-10: 0-7368-6723-6 (hardcover)
    1. Manatees—Juvenile literature. I. Title. II. Series.
QL737.S63R35 2007
599.55—dc22   2006020379

Editorial Credits
Martha E. H. Rustad, editor; Juliette Peters, set designer; Patrick D. Dentinger, book designer;
    Wanda Winch, photo researcher/photo editor

Photo Credits
Bruce Coleman Inc./P & R Hagan, 18–19
Jeff Rotman, 1
Kevin Schafer Photography, 14–15
Minden Pictures/Chris Newbert, cover, 16–17; Fred Bavendam, 8–9, 12–13; Norbert Wu, 20–21
Nature Picture Library/Doug Perrine, 10–11
Tom Stack & Associates, Inc./Brian Parker, 6–7; Tom Stack, 4–5

Note to Parents and Teachers

The Under the Sea set supports national science standards related to the diversity
and unity of life. This book describes and illustrates manatees. The images support
early readers in understanding the text. The repetition of words and phrases helps early
readers learn new words. This book also introduces early readers to subject-specific
vocabulary words, which are defined in the Glossary section. Early readers may need
assistance to read some words and to use the Table of Contents, Glossary, Read More,
Internet Sites, and Index sections of the book.

Printed in the United States of America in North Mankato, Minnesota.
092010   005956R

Table of Contents

What Are Manatees?

Manatees are water mammals.

They swim in seas and rivers.

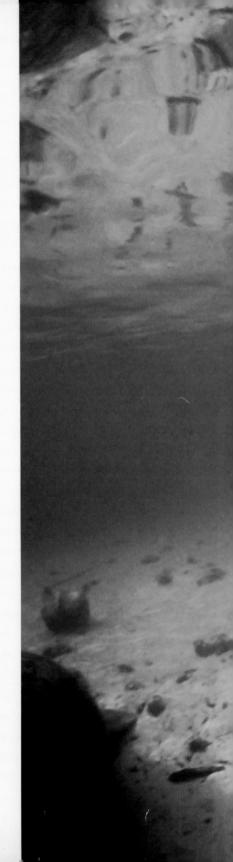

Manatees are about
the size of a large cow.
Manatees are sometimes
called sea cows.

Body Parts

Manatees have two flippers.

Manatees hold food up

to their mouths

with their flippers.

Manatees have

hundreds of whiskers.

Manatees feel

with their whiskers.

What Manatees Do

Manatees feel for plants
on the bottom of rivers
and bays.

Manatees eat the plants
they find.

Manatees flap their flat
tails up and down to swim.
Manatees swim slowly.

Manatees close their nostrils
when they are in the water.
They poke their nostrils
out of the water
to breathe air.

Manatees listen
for low sounds
from other manatees.
Manatees have small ears
that hear the sounds.

Under the Sea

Manatees spend their lives
in warm seas and rivers.

Glossary

bay—a part of the ocean that is partly closed in by land

flipper—a flat limb with bones; manatees use their flippers to swim and to hold food.

mammal—a warm-blooded animal that breathes air; mammals have hair or fur; female mammals feed milk to their young.

nostril—an opening in a nose through which one breathes air; manatees put their nostrils above the water to breathe air.

river—a large natural stream of fresh water that flows into lakes or oceans; manatees sometimes travel up rivers from the ocean.

whisker—a long hair near the mouth of an animal; manatees use their whiskers to feel for food.

Read More

Hirschmann, Kris. *Manatees.* Creatures of the Sea. Detroit: KidHaven Press, 2005.

Martin-James, Kathleen. *Gentle Manatees.* Pull Ahead Books. Minneapolis: Lerner, 2005.

Miller, Connie Colwell. *Manatees.* World of Mammals. Mankato, Minn.: Capstone Press, 2006.

Internet Sites

FactHound offers a safe, fun way to find Internet sites related to this book. All of the sites on FactHound have been researched by our staff.

Here's how:

1. Visit *www.facthound.com*

2. Choose your grade level.

3. Type in this book ID **0736867236** for age-appropriate sites. You may also browse subjects by clicking on letters, or by clicking on pictures and words.

4. Click on the **Fetch It** button.

FactHound will fetch the best sites for you!

Index

Word Count: 124
Grade: 1
Early-Intervention Level: 15

31901050751991